Arthur, the young knight, beamed in the moonlight. “Ah, the fair lady fears for my safety and tries to dissuade me from my dangerous journey! Dare I hope that she begins to favor me? I shall carry this morsel of encouragement in my heart to inspire my courage as I face the fiery breath of my enemy!”

“No, Arthur, wait! I need you here—”

“She needs me!” Arthur announced to the stars as he leaped onto his horse. “Fear not, fair Sabrina! For I shall return to your arms victorious before the moon wanes!”

“Arthur, wait! No!” Her heart sank as she watched him gallop off in the moonlight. He was her champion, and she needed his help to figure out how to get out of this place and back home, where she belonged.

“Guess he couldn’t hear you through all that armor,” Salem commented as he leaped to the windowsill. Then he giggled and added, “I never knew you were into heavy metal, Sabrina.”

Titles in Sabrina, the Teenage Witch™ Pocket Books series:

#1 Sabrina, the Teenage Witch
#2 Showdown at the Mall
#3 Good Switch, Bad Switch
#4 Halloween Havoc
#5 Santa's Little Helper
#6 Ben There, Done That
#7 All You Need Is a Love Spell
#8 Salem on Trial
#9 A Dog's Life
#10 Lotsa Luck
#11 Prisoner of Cabin 13
#12 All That Glitters
#13 Go Fetch!
#14 Spying Eyes
Sabrina Goes to Rome
#15 Harvest Moon
#16 Now You See Her, Now You Don't
#17 Eight Spells a Week *(Super Edition)*
#18 I'll Zap Manhattan
#19 Shamrock Shenanigans
#20 Age of Aquariums
#21 Prom Time
#22 Witchopoly
#23 Bridal Bedlam
#24 Scarabian Nights
#25 While the Cat's Away
#26 Fortune Cookie Fox
#27 Haunts in the House
Sabrina Down Under
#28 Up, Up, and Away
Sabrina's Guide to the Universe
#29 Millennium Madness *(Super Edition)*
#30 Switcheroo
#31 Mummy Dearest
#32 Reality Check
#33 Knock on Wood
#34 It's a Miserable Life!
#35 Pirate Pandemonium
#36 Wake-Up Call
#37 Witch Way Did She Go?
#38 Milady's Dragon
#39 From the Horse's Mouth
#40 Dream Boat
#41 Tiger Tale
#42 The Witch That Launched a Thousand Ships
#43 Know It All
#44 Topsy-Turvy
#45 Hounded by Baskervilles

Milady's Dragon

Cathy East Dubowski

Based upon the characters in Archie Comics

And based upon the television series
Sabrina, The Teenage Witch
Created for television by Nell Scovell
Developed for television by Jonathan Schmock

POCKET
BOOKS

LONDON • SYDNEY • NEW YORK • TOKYO • SINGAPORE • TORONTO

First published in Great Britain in 2001 by Pocket Books
An imprint of Simon & Schuster UK Ltd
Africa House, 64-78 Kingsway
London WC2B 6AH

First published in 2001 by Simon Pulse,
An imprint of Simon & Schuster
Children's Publishing Division, New York

A CIP catalogue record for this book is
available from the British Library

ISBN 0 7434 0421 1

1 3 5 7 9 10 8 6 4 2

Printed and bound in Great Britain by
Bookmarque Ltd, Croydon, Surrey

To my two best friends,
Miladies Lauren and Megan

Milady's Dragon

Chapter 1

Sabrina Spellman couldn't wait. She was starving.

As she put her car in drive to pull away from the drive-through window, she dug her hand into one of the bags for a French fry . . .

And pulled out a long stick of charred spud.

She stared at it a minute, arguing with her stomach about how desperate it was for food.

"Not that hungry." With a sigh, she glanced in her rearview mirror. Luckily the driver behind her was busy putting on mascara and hadn't pulled up to the drive-through window yet. Sabrina put her car in reverse and very, very carefully inched her way back to the window.

"Um, excuse me . . ."

The bored-looking kid in the goofy hat looked at her blankly.

"Hello?" She tried again.

"You're going the wrong way."

"I know—I mean, I had to back up. You see, I have a little problem with my order. . . ." She smiled as she reached for the bag—a smile the fast-food guy didn't return.

She held the bag of burned fries up to the window. "Sorry, but my fries—they're kind of . . . well, burned a little."

The burger guy didn't reach for the bag, just peeked in, then shrugged.

The driver in the car behind her honked.

"You're holding up the line," the burger guy said.

"But—but what about my fries?" Sabrina asked.

"What about 'em?"

"Well, look at them. They're burned."

The guy shrugged again. "Most people like them crisp."

"Crisp?" Sabrina exclaimed. "They look like they were cooked by a fire-breathing dragon!"

"Well, ex-cuuuse me," the guy said. With an irritated frown, he snatched the bag from her hand and slowly, very slowly, walked over to the hot-food tray.

The driver behind her leaned on the horn.

"Take it easy," Sabrina muttered. "Like, put on some blush or something." Of course, she didn't say it so the driver could hear—she was much too polite.

What seemed like ten minutes later, the burger guy came back to the window and without a word held out a new bag.

"Thanks," Sabrina said politely.

"Can I take your order?" he mumbled into the microphone, dismissing her as he addressed the next customer.

Honk! Honk! Ho-o-o-o-onk!

Sabrina stared at the burger guy. She really couldn't believe it. No apology for the burned food, no thank you for buying food here, no "you're welcome" to her thanks. Whatever happened to customer service? Good manners? Half-human behavior? "Why do I even come to these places?" she wondered miserably as she pulled away from the window.

"Because you needed the car," said a voice from the backseat.

Sabrina nearly ran into a telephone pole by the exit. "Salem?" she asked, her heart pounding.

"In the fur," said the Spellmans' sleek black warlock-turned-cat. When he'd tried to take over the world a few years back, the Witches' Council turned Salem Saberhagen into a cat and took away all his powers. All, that is, except one—the ability to talk.

"Don't *do* that," Sabrina complained as she tried to make her heart stop pounding. "You scared me half to death."

"My sincerest apologies."

"What are you doing in the car?"

"Escaping."

"Escaping what?"

"Your aunts," Salem replied as he leaped up into the front seat beside her. "They're at it again. Bickering like two little girls. You'd think they were six years old instead of six *hundred.* And you remember how that is, Sabrina. When they get like that, they're miserable to live with."

"You mean, they're too busy arguing to pay you any attention," Sabrina guessed with a half smile.

"Well . . . it would be nice if you could scratch my tummy," he admitted pitifully as he sprawled back against the seat.

When Sabrina stopped at a red light, she reached over and gave Salem's tummy a good rub. She did remember what it was like when her aunts fought. She'd been living on her own for a year now, in a house she shared with three roommates—Morgan, Miles, and Roxie. But she'd lived with her aunts for several years while learning to be a witch, and they'd been wonderful—except when their sibling rivalry got a little intense.

"You're right," Sabrina said. "I did need the car." Roxie had loaned her her car, but only if she promised to bring back dinner for everyone. Sabrina could have just used a little magic to whip up some burgers, but Roxie had insisted on burgers from her favorite fast-food restaurant. Witches couldn't do brand names—it was a trademark issue the Witches' Council hadn't worked out yet—only equivalent substitutions. Sabrina thought Roxie might have a problem if she brought back food from Burger Queen.

"So what'd you get?" Salem asked, pawing at the bags. "Any fish sandwiches?"

"Paws off!" Sabrina warned. "I've got three starving roommates back at the house, and I had to wait in line for thirty minutes to get this stuff."

"But . . ."

"Here," Sabrina said, and pointed at the seat in front of Salem's twitchy little nose. A tiny square box appeared in a wave of sparkles.

"Pizza 'Hot'?" Salem asked.

"Anchovy," Sabrina replied.

That was all it took. For the rest of the drive home, the car was blissfully quiet as Salem the cat pigged out.

As she parked the car outside her house, Salem burped loudly.

Sabrina winced. "I'll pretend we're in China and you meant that as a thank you." She got out of the car and reached for the bags of food. Salem leaped to the ground beside her and began to follow her to the front door.

"And just what do you think you're doing?" she asked.

"Inviting myself to stay with you for a while?" Salem said hopefully.

Sabrina sighed. "All right. But keep out of sight."

"Don't worry," Salem assured her. "Your roommates kind of scare me."

Sabrina carried the food into the house and dumped it out on the table. The doors to her roommates' rooms were closed, as usual, but in about ten seconds, as the smell of food reached them, Morgan, Miles, and Roxie barged out of their rooms and pounced on the food.

"Hey, these fries are raw," Miles complained.

"You're kidding!" Sabrina reached for the French fry he was holding. Ewww! As limp as a wet noodle. She couldn't believe it! "Um, I think there are more in the bag," Sabrina said.

Surreptitiously, she flicked her finger at one of the bulging bags. She couldn't conjure up more bags of the real thing, but she could sure crisp up what was there. "Better?" she asked as Miles pulled out another bag.

"They're okay," Miles muttered with his mouth full of food.

Sabrina looked away.

"Hey, where's my apple turnover?" Morgan complained. "You forgot, didn't you?"

"No, I promise, I ordered it." Sabrina dumped out every bag but couldn't find any turnovers.

Sabrina glanced at her housemate. Morgan could be a tough cookie on a good day. Sabrina wasn't in the mood to see her explode into flames over a turnover.

Zap! An empty bag suddenly bulged with food. "Ah, here they are!" She removed a turnover from the bag and held it out to Morgan.

Morgan peered curiously at the wrapper. "Burger Que—?"

"Let me get you a plate!" Sabrina said quickly as she dashed to the kitchen cabinets. She slipped the turnover onto a plate and quickly balled up the Burger Queen wrapper.

Roxie scooped up all her food and glanced at the cups of soda. "So, which one is diet?" she asked.

Uh-oh. Sabrina realized she'd only ordered regular sodas.

Like, why would it matter if you're eating eight

thousand calories worth of burgers and fries? Sabrina picked up a cup and pressed down the little circle by the word *Diet.* "Here you go," she said, crossing her fingers behind her back.

Roxie snatched up the cup, then, like clockwork, all three of Sabrina's housemates retreated to their rooms.

Three doors slammed in unison.

"You're welcome," she sang out.

Silence.

With a sigh Sabrina sat down at the table and poked among the bags and wrappers, looking for her own dinner. But the only thing left was a single bag of half-cooked, grease-soaked fries. "Great," she muttered. With a glance over her shoulder, she used her magic to whip up some more food. "I guess Burger Queen will have to do. . . ."

Friday nights at the coffee house where Sabrina worked part-time were usually busy, but tonight was worse than usual. Sabrina could have zapped herself into twins and still would have had trouble keeping everybody happy.

"Hey, waitress!" an older man with a mustache called out. "Where's my double skinny latte?"

"Coming!" she said with a smile.

Josh laid out a tray of coffees and pastries. "Sabrina, take this over to those kids by the door, okay?" he said. "And they didn't pay yet, so make sure you get their money." He glanced at the receipt. "It's sixteen ninety-five."

"No problem." Sabrina scooped up the tray and carried it over to the table of three guys and two girls. They were all laughing and talking and horsing around.

"That'll be sixteen ninety-five," she said as she set the drinks and food on the table.

"Hey, it's your turn, Art!" one of the boys yelled. "I paid last time."

"No way," the guy named Art replied. "I'm paying for the movie, remember?" He turned to his friend and punched him in the arm. "You are so overdue, Jeremy. *You* pay."

The girls giggled as Jeremy pulled out his wallet and shook it upside down. "I'm skinned, man." He glanced up at Sabrina. "I'm going to have to run down to the ATM and get some cash. Can we pay you in a few minutes?"

Sabrina smiled. "Sure, no problem. I'll catch you before you leave."

"Oh, miss! Miss!" a woman called from the counter. "You're out of napkins!"

"Oh, sorry." Sabrina hurried over and checked under the counter. Darn, no napkins. "I'm sorry," she told the woman as she stood back up again. "I'll have to get some more from the back room."

The woman frowned. "Well, can you hurry? I think my cup's leaking."

Sabrina hurried into the back room and searched for more napkins.

By the time she came back, the woman was gone. Sabrina refilled the napkin holder, then started to take the next order.

That's when she saw them.

Or rather, didn't see them.

The kids by the front door—the ones who hadn't paid yet, the ones who had to hit the cash machine to pay—were gone.

Maybe they left their money on the table, since I was in the back room, she thought. As soon as she helped the last customer, she hurried over to the table.

As she searched among the napkins and clutter, her heart sank. She didn't see any money anywhere. Had they sneaked out without paying?

Just then she spotted an envelope with the words "A Tip for the Waitress" written on the outside.

Sabrina smiled in relief and reached for it. But when she opened it, she didn't see any money at all. There was only a note scribbled on a sheet of paper:

Here's your tip:

Make your customers pay up front.

Darn! They had skipped out. *How rude!*

Sabrina ran through the door of the coffee house and out to the sidewalk, hoping to catch them.

The streets were crowded with people out for a Friday night of entertainment, but she didn't see the kids anywhere.

Jerks! She thought as she went back into the coffee shop. Angry, she cleaned up their table. On top of everything they'd left a terrible mess of wadded-up napkins and paper airplanes and coffee spills.

As she carried a tray of dirty cups and trash back to the bar, Josh came over with a worried frown. "Sabrina, what happened? Are you all right?"

She guessed he'd seen her run out of the coffee house. "I'm fine. I tried to chase down some kids who left without paying. I'm sorry, Josh. I should have insisted they pay. I should've kept an eye on them—"

"Don't worry about it," Josh said with a smile. "It's not the first time it's happened here." He shook his head. "It'd be one thing if it was a homeless person or somebody really hungry and broke, but it's usually rich college kids who shouldn't have any problem paying."

"Excuse me!" a tall blond girl at the takeout section of the counter called out in a sarcastic tone. "Are you guys like open or what?"

Sabrina's finger twitched as she felt an overwhelming desire to turn the girl into a cockroach. Josh must have noticed the look on her face, because he stepped in front of her and whispered so the girl couldn't hear, "Smile, Sabrina. Remember, the customer is always right."

"Yeah, right." Sabrina stuffed her hands into the pockets of her jeans and tried to smile. *Wrong! Where have all the nice people gone?* she wondered as she carried her tray of dirty dishes to the dishwasher.

☆

Chapter 2

☆

Saturday started out even worse.

She'd run by her aunts' house to get some things out of her old room to take to her new quarters.

Somehow this put her aunts in a bad mood.

Aunt Zelda and Aunt Hilda weren't agreeing on anything this morning—except Sabrina's weekly list of mistakes.

"When I was your age . . ." Aunt Zelda kept saying.

"When you were my age, it was the Middle Ages," Sabrina finally said. "For one thing, things were a lot simpler. There was a lot less history to learn for midterms!"

"—And we did not talk back to our elders," Zelda pointed out.

"I wasn't talking back!" Sabrina protested.

"See?" Hilda said to Zelda. "She's doing it again."

"I—" Sabrina closed her mouth and gave up. No use arguing. She knew what was really going on.

Her aunts missed her. And they were getting on each other's nerves. And they were taking it out on her.

It sort of made sense, in a weird way.

"So anyone want to come with me to the Faire today?" Sabrina asked, hoping it would end the arguing for a while. "It's a Medieval Faire—a weekend-long reenactment of life in the Middle Ages."

"Been there, done that," Hilda said with a scowl.

"I thought you had a big history midterm to study for," Zelda chided.

"So? I can do research for my exam *and* have one of those giant turkey legs. It's a win/win."

Salem bounded into the room. "Did someone mention oversized poultry?" He licked his lips at the thought.

Aunt Zelda looked at Sabrina with the tiniest pout. "You could have asked me for information about the Middle Ages. I'm primary research. I was there. I know what really happened."

"I didn't want to bother you," Sabrina fibbed. Actually she'd thought about it, but she wasn't sure her aunts would give her an unbiased account.

"It's no bother." Aunt Zelda sat down at the

kitchen table with a cup of tea. "What would you like to ask me?"

"Actually," Sabrina said, "what I'd really like to ask you is, Do you guys have anything I can wear? It's always more fun if you wear period dress."

Hilda shook her head. "I got rid of all those old rags. Too out of it. Too restricting. Too—"

"Tight?" Zelda suggested.

"Well, who didn't put on a few pounds during the Renaissance?" Hilda asked.

"Sabrina, I think I have a few things that might fit you," Aunt Zelda said. "But . . . well, are you sure you can borrow one without getting any junk food on it?"

Hilda rolled her eyes. "Just because I spilled a tiny little drop of mulled wine on that dress I borrowed from you in 1597—"

"Tiny drop?" Zelda exclaimed. "It was as if you'd gone swimming in a moat."

"That's not true!" Hilda exclaimed indignantly. "And besides, it was a tacky dress anyway—"

"Really? Then why were you so anxious to borrow it?"

"Aunt Zelda! Aunt Hilda!" Sabrina exclaimed, stepping between her aunts.

The two Spellman sisters stopped arguing but continued to stare daggers at each other over their niece's head.

"I promise to take very good care of your dress, Aunt Zelda," Sabrina said.

Zelda smiled at her. "I'm sure you will, dear. Come on, then, let's go look at—"

Thunk! The toaster popped. All three witches jumped, because the toaster didn't just make toast, it also received messages from the Other Realm. Usually very important ones.

"Well, Hilda. Go on. Open it," Zelda told her sister.

Hilda stepped back, staring at the toaster as if it might come alive and bite her. "You open it, Zelda. *You're* the oldest."

Zelda glared. "Thanks for the reminder." Reluctantly she snatched the message from the toaster and laid it out on the table to read.

" 'Urgent,' it says. 'Rush.' " Zelda looked up at her sister. "There's an urgent meeting of the Witches' Council." Zelda bit her nail, obviously concerned. "Sabrina, I'm sorry. We'll have to talk about your history paper later. We have to fly." With a flick of her hands, she changed into a chic powder-blue suit with matching heels and slipped her reading glasses into an elegant leather briefcase. She gave her sister the once-over. "Is *that* what you're wearing?"

Hilda glanced down at her black jeans and "Elvis Lives!" T-shirt. "What's wrong with what

I'm wearing?" She pouted and looked at Sabrina. "She's always made fun of my clothes, even when we were teenagers. What do you think, Sabrina? Do you think this is okay for a meeting of the Witches' Council?"

"Uh, I . . . um . . ." Sabrina hated to get caught in the middle of her aunts' little "debates."

"No time to argue over clothes," Zelda interrupted, and with a swirl of her hand and a point of her beautifully manicured finger, she instantly changed Hilda's clothes into a similar suit, this one tailored of champagne-beige linen.

"Ugh!" Hilda exclaimed, staring down at herself.

"Charming," Zelda pronounced as she dragged her sister toward the stairs.

"But I don't want charming," Hilda protested. "Charming is boring. I want something . . . interesting." And with a snap of her fingers, she changed the chic suit into a long, flowing Indian print dress.

Zelda rolled her eyes and pointed her finger again. "Charming!" And zapped her sister back into the beige suit.

And so it went, back and forth, as the two aunts hurried up the staircase.

"But, Aunt Zelda! What about the dress for me?" Sabrina called up the stairs.

"Oh, of course. Yes, well, dear. Let me tell you where it is," Zelda called back down. "It's up in the attic, in that little closet near the front window. Help yourself. Just promise me you'll take care of it. The clothes of my youth hold a great deal of sentimental value for me."

"Thanks, Aunt Zelda. I promise. And I bet I'll be the only girl there wearing an authentic dress from the actual Middle Ages."

"Knowing Zelda's taste, you'll probably look middle-aged," Hilda snapped as Zelda prodded her up the stairs.

The two sisters continued to bicker as they stood in front of the linen closet—their quick shuttle to the Other Realm. Seconds after they had stepped in amid the towels and bargain-sized bottles of shampoo and shut the door, thunder shook the old Victorian home and lightning flashed—

And Sabrina knew they'd been safely—and instantly—transported to the Other Realm.

Beats the subway any day, Sabrina thought as she hurried up the stairs.

Once she reached the landing, she headed to the end of the hall and opened a door. Another set of steep winding stairs led up to the attic, where her aunts stored relics from centuries of living in the mortal world. A small window let in light as Sabrina carefully stepped around boxes and trunks, old lamps, and furniture that could easily have fetched a fortune at an antiques auction.

Near the window she found a huge old carved wardrobe. Inside hung dozens of gowns from various periods of history. *Looks like the costume room in the drama department at school,* Sabrina thought.

One by one she examined them. Several looked perfect for a day at a Medieval Faire. But then she spotted a dress in a clear garment bag almost hidden at the end of the overstuffed wardrobe. The color—deep ruby red—caught her eye. She lugged out the garment bag and quickly unzipped it.

"It's beautiful . . ." Sabrina breathed as she touched the luxurious red fabric. Eagerly she changed out of her jeans and T-shirt and slipped the beautiful gown over her head. Instantly she felt as elegant as a lady of the court, and she was thrilled to find that the dress fit her perfectly. She hurried over to a tall standing mirror to see how it looked. "Oh, wow!" she exclaimed as she twirled before the mirror. She couldn't help but smile at her appearance. What girl could wear such a dress and not feel like a princess? "It's wonderful!" she exclaimed as she ran her hand down a rich velvet sleeve.

And then she stopped. She felt something, a small strange lump in the fabric on the inside of her forearm. She examined the sleeve more closely and realized that a hidden pocket had been sewn into it. And there was something in it!

Sabrina quickly pulled out the object and gasped in delight—it was a dazzling gold necklace with an emerald the size of a quarter! She slipped it over her head and then glanced in the mirror to see how it looked with the gown.

"Perfect!" Sabrina exclaimed. She was sure Aunt Zelda wouldn't mind if she wore the necklace, too. Besides, she told herself, it couldn't be a real emerald, it was too large. It had to be costume jewelry.

Sabrina closed the wardrobe and hurried downstairs to get her purse, a black velvet sack that didn't look half bad with her outfit. She doubted medieval women carried handbags, but hey, she had to make a little concession to the modern world.

She spotted Salem sunning himself on a windowsill in the living room. "So, Salem, how do I look?"

"A bit overdressed for the mall," was his catty remark.

"Very funny," Sabrina said. "So, are you ready to rumble?"

"A good joust beats those WWF clowns any

day." Salem stretched and stood up. "Just get me a dozen or so turkey legs, then you can go wherever you want."

"Eww." Sabrina scunched up her nose.

Sabrina started to say no. Salem could be a pain sometimes—actually, a lot of the time!—but then again, she hadn't spent much time with him since she'd gone off to college and moved into the house. And Aunt Zelda and Aunt Hilda were gone for who knew how long—Other Realm time didn't translate exactly to the clocks of the mortal realm. Salem could be alone for a long time. Poor kitty . . .

Salem looked up at her like a kitty from a cat-food commercial.

"Oh, all right, you can come. . . ." Sabrina said, and Salem leaped happily into her arms.

"Hang on tight!" she exclaimed, and with a quick snap of her fingers they took the express line to the Faire.

Sunlight streamed through the trees, casting dappled patterns on the forest floor as Sabrina followed the rest of the crowd down a wooded path. Music beckoned them from the Medieval Faire beyond a pair of gates.

It was a beautiful day, and many of the people around her were dressed in period costumes. It was easy to imagine that she had actually been sent back in time.

Especially after she paid her fee and entered the gates.

A sign on the gates advised:

All ye who pass through these gates—
Forget the troubles of the modern world, and let your hearts transport you back in time to a place where every maid was a lady to be fought for, and every man a gallant knight in shining armor.

"I'm definitely up for this," Sabrina said as she made her way down the path.

"I'm hungry," Salem said.

Sabrina laughed. "Salem, do you ever think of anything besides your stomach?"

Salem thought a moment as he trotted along beside her. "Yes, on Thursdays between nine and twelve. That's when I routinely review my portfolio with my bookie, uh, stockbroker."

Soon the path opened up into a large clearing in the forest—and it was a fantastic scene. "It's like something out of a movie!" Sabrina exclaimed.

Colorful pennants flew in the air. Men and women in bright costumes beckoned to fairgoers from their stalls as they offered their wares:

everything from meat pies to wreaths of ribbons and flowers for young girls to wear in their hair.

Without any prodding from Salem, Sabrina stopped at a stall to taste some authentic food. "What will you have, fair maiden?" a jolly woman asked. "How about one of my famous meat pies and a stein of cider?"

Sabrina studied the woman's wares and decided to try a couple of the flaky turnover-like meat pies. She paid her money, then bit into one. "Mmm, what are these?" she asked through a mouthful of food.

"Pigeon pies," the woman said with a twinkle in her eye.

"Bleh!" Sabrina spit out the food onto the ground as the woman laughed uproariously. Was the woman teasing? Sabrina couldn't tell. But she decided she'd stick to her cider and an apple dumpling.

"If you're not going to eat that . . ." Salem volunteered, whipping his tail in the air.

As they strolled along, two jugglers walked by, delighting the crowd with acrobatic tricks and juggling everything from apples to flaming torches.

A wandering minstrel ambled by, singing a tale of courtly love. "Ahh, I remember when that tune hit number one," Salem said with a nostalgic tear in his eye.

And a maiden wandered through the crowd selling bags of herbs guaranteed to snare the true love of one's choice.

At one stall Sabrina tried on one of the flower-and-ribbon wreaths in her hair. "Aye, but ye be a fair lass," the man teased her as he held up a mirror for her to see. "Ye should head over to the tournament," he added with a wink. "Ye'll find more than yer share of handsome knights over there just waitin' to joust for the hand of a lady as fair as ye."

Sabrina laughed at his flirtatious sales pitch and gladly paid for the flowered headpiece.

As she headed for the tournament area, she picked up her skirts as she came to a muddy area that she had to cross in order to reach the stands. *I'd better be careful,* she thought, *or I'll ruin Aunt Zelda's gown.*

Before she could take one step across the muddy grass, one of the costumed actors dashed in front of her and cast his cape on the ground. "Milady," he said as he went down on one knee and bowed his head. "The sight of your beauty wounds me—and I could not bear it if I allowed myself to stand by and watch you ruin your beautiful gown. Please, tread upon my worthless cape and be borne across this foul ground unsullied."

Sabrina's hand flew to her mouth to smother her giggles. *I was definitely born in the wrong century,* she thought, smiling down at the handsome, gallant young man. Behind her she heard Salem gag as if he were choking on a hairball, but she just ignored him. "But, my kind sir," she replied, getting into the act. " 'Twould wound me to spoil the cape of one so noble as you. Ye."

The handsome young man looked up at her and winked, delighted to have her go along with his masquerade. "Never fear, milady. I have several more freshly laundered ones back at the costume tent."

"Oh, well, then—cool." Smiling, Sabrina lifted her skirts and marched across the cape, then laughed when she realized that Salem was trotting across the cape behind her. Salem hated getting muddy almost as much as he hated getting wet.

"My kitty and I both thank you, kind sir."

"It was an honor," the young man replied as he bent to kiss her hand.

"Hmm, I could get to like this," Sabrina couldn't help but say.

"Me, too," the guy replied as he stood up again. "So, do you, like, go to school around here or something?"

"Adams."

"Really? Me, too. I'm supposed to be premed,

but as you can see"—he swept a hand along his costume and chuckled—"my heart's in the drama department."

"Acting can be good medicine," Sabrina said. "Or is that laughter? Anyway, you know what I mean."

"Yeah. So what about you?"

"Journalism," Sabrina answered. "But I'm taking all kinds of classes at this point. I like to try new things."

"So," he said, wiggling his eyebrows up and down, "interested in trying out a new guy?"

Sabrina laughed. "Maybe—if he's as gallant in the modern world as he is here in the past."

"Oh—he is! I mean—I am," he promised with such sweet earnestness that Sabrina figured he just might be. He scribbled down his cell phone number and handed it to Sabrina. "Maybe we could get together for a study date or something next week."

Sabrina smiled. "That would be nice. Oh—and I'm Sabrina, by the way. What's your name?"

"Would you believe . . . Lance?" the guy said sheepishly.

"No. You're kidding. Really?"

"Really," he said, blushing. "You'd think with a name like that, I'd have landed a job as a jouster. Oh, well." He looked around. "Well, fair maiden," he said, returning to his role, "I'd best be off in search of other lasses to charm, or I might find myself demoted to the role of blacksmith's apprentice." He picked up his muddy cape and held it out at arm's length. "Farewell, fair Sabrina," he called as he hurried off. "And don't forget to call me!"

"Bye, Lance!" Sabrina called after him.

"Teenagers!" Salem muttered as he made another gagging sound.

"Oh, hush, Salem. He was sweet—a lot sweeter than most of the ogres I've been running into lately."

They wandered toward the tournament grounds, where many kinds of games were in progress. She watched in amazement as an archer time after time hit the bull's-eye of his target.

Suddenly Salem spotted the turkey leg stand and ran off. Without thinking, Sabrina dashed after him and scooped him up—just as the archer let fly one of his arrows.

In the blink of a witch's eyelash, Sabrina hugged Salem to her chest and muttered a spell at the speed of light—so fast she wasn't even sure she spoke it aloud:

Oh, fair medieval lady,
Far may you roam,

But make a quick wish
That will carry you home.

The noonday sun flashed on the emerald of her necklace . . .

And one half-second later she saw the arrow flying toward her . . .

Sabrina felt herself disappear.

Chapter 3

Sabrina landed with a hard *thump!*

"Ow!" Salem moaned, *not* landing on his feet.

Sabrina sprawled on the ground a moment, savoring the sensation of not having an arrow piercing her chest, and fought to catch her breath.

"Whoa," she said to Salem, "that's the fastest spell I ever cast in my life. I can't believe it worked. But thank goodness it did."

"Warn me next time," Salem whined as he got to his feet.

"If I had taken the time this time," Sabrina replied, "you and I might have been a Sabrina/Salem shish kebab. Just be thankful we're both safe."

"Okay," Salem said. "I'm thankful. Next topic: Where exactly are we?"

"Home, I guess. That's where I asked to be sent in the spell." But as she looked around, Sabrina realized she didn't know where she was. She definitely wasn't home at her aunts' Victorian house in Westbridge, or at her house with her three roommates.

In fact, she and Salem were in the middle of some dense woods.

"Okay, we're lost in some forest, where there might be something that likes to eat cats," Salem said, worried. "So, could you get us out of here?"

"Don't worry," Sabrina said. But before she could do anything, they heard the sound of horse's hooves pounding through the thick forest . . .

"Listen," Salem whispered. "He's coming this way!" Trembling, the black cat darted behind a tree.

Sabrina ducked behind a tree just as a person on horseback rode into the clearing. She heard metal clank as the rider jumped to the ground.

"Hello there!" a voice called out.

When Sabrina didn't speak or move, he shouted, "Show yourself—now!—or be introduced to the wicked blade of my sword!"

"There's nobody here!" Salem squeaked.

Sabrina winced.

"Wait a minute," the man said. "If nobody's

there, who's talking? And what's this!" he shouted triumphantly.

Sabrina squealed as she felt herself being tugged from her hiding place by the hem of her gown. By the time she was out in the clearing, her dress was up to her knee.

The man who'd grabbed her gasped and let go of her gown, then dropped to his knee. "Fair lady, forgive me! I—I meant you no harm!"

Heart pounding, Sabrina smoothed down her dress and studied the person who knelt before her. He was young, maybe twenty or so, and dressed in a suit of shining armor that looked like something out of a museum. His thick black hair fell over his brow as a blush the color of her gown spread across his cheeks.

Sabrina swallowed and tried to calm her racing heart. This cute hunk was obviously part of the Medieval Faire, playing out a part, like Lance. And he looked vaguely familiar. But she supposed she'd just seen him around the fairgrounds somewhere. She felt quite foolish that she'd hidden in fear.

"Um, stand up, Sir Knight," she began, still embarrassed by her actions.

The young knight stood, his eyes lowered. But she noticed he checked out her leg, which was now covered by the rich ruby material of her dress.

"Forgive me, fair lady," the knight repeated. "But I've been attacked several times on my journey." He stared at her then with eyes of a startling blue. "Are you in distress?" he asked hastily.

"Me?" Sabrina glanced around. "Oh, no, I'm fine. Really."

The knight looked puzzled. "But how come you to be here all alone, in the forest?"

Sabrina laughed a little self-consciously. "I guess I just wandered away from the Faire. Um, would you mind telling me which way the ticket booth is? Or the exit gate?"

"Ticket booth?" the knight asked, confused. "Exit gate?"

"Yeah. Don't get me wrong—I've had a great time. I mean, it's been a total blast. But I need to get home and hit the books."

"Blast?" the knight asked, still looking puzzled. "Hit . . . books?"

Sabrina sighed. Okay, so this guy was determined not to act out of character. But really, she needed some help. "Do you know where I can find Lance?" she asked. "Or how I can get out of here?"

The knight slowly shook his head. "I know of no one by the name of Lance. But I can help you get to a safe place." He glanced around. "Are you alone, fair lady?"

"Yeah. Except for my cat." She looked behind

the tree. "Salem—come on, it's time to go. It's okay to come out."

"Are you sure?" Salem whispered.

"Yes!" Sabrina whispered, then said more loudly, "Here, kitty, kitty. Come out, come out, wherever you are."

At last Salem trotted into the clearing and jumped into Sabrina's arms.

"So, lead the way," Sabrina said brightly.

The knight looked shocked. "Why, it is much too far for a lady to walk," he said. "You must ride."

Hmm. Sabrina looked up at the knight's fine horse. She wasn't exactly an experienced rider, but she guessed she could hang on. "Um, okay. Can you help me get up on this thing?"

The knight bowed, then easily lifted Sabrina to sit sidesaddle on the horse. With great attention he adjusted her skirts so they covered her legs completely.

Then the knight swung up onto the horse behind her and reached around her to gather the reins.

Sabrina blushed in spite of herself at the feel of his arms around her. He was quite a hunk after all.

"I am Arthur of Kensington Keep, knight in training," he introduced himself as they rode.

"I'm Sabrina. Thanks a lot for helping me out."

"It is my sworn duty to be the champion of all fair ladies such as you," he said simply.

"Cool," Sabrina said.

"I'm sorry I have no cloak to warm you with," he said sorrowfully, "but the only one I had was destroyed in my last battle with wayside thieves."

Sabrina glanced nervously around. Wayside thieves? She hoped they weren't going to do one of those reenactment things with her in the middle of it. Stuff like that freaked her out, even when she knew it was staged.

"I'm fine," Sabrina said politely.

"The journey is not a long one by horse," he informed her. "I shall hurry as fast as is comfortable for milady's ride."

"Uh, thanks."

They rode most of the way in silence. Arthur rarely spoke except to ask about Sabrina's comfort or health.

He was definitely a gentleman, and Sabrina had to admit she enjoyed the knightly behavior.

"So when are we getting out of here?" Salem finally whispered.

"Shh!" Sabrina whispered back. "And don't worry, I'm sure we're almost there."

"Milady, is everything all right? Why do you talk to your cat?"

"Oh, uh, I am far away from home, and it gives me comfort to talk to him," she improvised.

The knight nodded. "I had a pig like that once," he said sadly. "But . . . we had to eat him."

Sabrina didn't have a response to that, so she just nodded sadly. Salem's claws tightened on her arm.

Soon Arthur announced, "The village is up ahead, milady. We shall be there soon."

Sabrina squinted to see through the forest. She could barely see anything, but then she saw what looked like some buildings. Soon they rode into what looked like a tiny medieval village. Sabrina supposed, she hadn't been to this part of the Medieval Faire, because she didn't see anything familiar.

The knight slowed his horse and dismounted near a meat pie vendor's stall. Smiling up at her, he held out his hand and helped her get down. He even gave Salem a gentle pat and laid him at Sabrina's feet. "Now, milady, may I help you find your family? Your father, or brother?"

"Oh, I just came here by myself," she said, then stepped back at the look of horror on his face.

"Alone?" he gasped. "Why, that's . . . that's foolhardy, milady. You must never travel alone." He bowed low before her amazed eyes. "I vow never to leave your side until I've delivered you to one of your kin."

"Really, that's not necessary," Sabrina said. "Look, I'm enjoying the game. I mean, you're terrific, but you're taking things a little too far. Just point me to the front entrance and I'm out of here."

"What is this front entrance you speak of?" Arthur asked.

"Look, I appreciate all the help, and how polite you are and all, but I just need to get home and I can get there all by myself. So, thanks for everything. Well, gotta go!"

"But, milady—"

Sabrina didn't stick around to argue with the guy. She hoisted her skirts—as beautiful as the dress was, it was a pain to run in—and dashed across the village with Salem at her heels. *I'll just ask somebody else,* she decided. *Somebody who isn't so tied up playing his part. Or I'll just keep looking till I find my way out of here myself. . . .*

Sabrina sniffed. *Ewww, the place really reeks,* she thought as she glanced around. She noticed a few animals wallowing in some garbage. And some of the actors . . . *Well, let's just say they've been out in the hot sun and away from the showers for a little too long,* Sabrina thought politely.

They didn't have to make the place that authentic!

"Sabrina, slow down!" Salem panted. "I—*gasp*—need to ask you something."

Sabrina slowed down and looked behind her. There was no sign of Arthur. *The armor probably slows him down,* she guessed. "So, what's your question?" she asked Salem.

"Why are we looking for the front gate?" Salem asked. "Just point and shoot us home."

"Okay," Sabrina replied. "I just don't like to do it in a crowd. And," she added thoughtfully, "I'm not sure why it didn't work the first time."

"Maybe there was some interference or something," Salem suggested. "Like solar flares or cell phone rays. And you did spout off that spell awfully fast. Maybe it was just enough magic to get us out of the way of the arrow, but not enough to send us home."

"Hmm, you may be right."

"Come on, Sabrina. I'm starving—"

"Again?"

"All this running around burns calories, you know," he replied huffily. "And I've had enough excitement for one day. There's a pillow in front of the TV and a bowl of Kitty Snax calling me."

"Okay, okay. But come on, Salem. Over here." She led him behind some bushes, then lifted him into her arms. "Hold on tight, Salem. Ow! Not that tight! You'll ruin Aunt Zelda's dress!"

Salem withdrew his claws.

"Okay, let's see.

Medieval lady, all alone,
Point your finger and hurry home.

Sabrina pointed and closed her eyes as she felt a jolt—a good sign the spell was working.

But when she opened her eyes, she was still in the middle of the same village.

Sabrina frowned. "I don't get it. My magic feels like it's working, but it's not."

"Maybe you messed up because you're not actually alone," Salem suggested helpfully. "I'm with you, too, you know. And 'alone,' 'home'—well, it's not Dr. Seuss, is it?"

"Thanks for the critique," Sabrina said dryly. "You know, it's not so easy to make up poetry when you're in a hurry—and when you've got a crabby cat in your arms distracting you."

"Sor-ry," Salem said. "I was just trying to be helpful. Come on, try again. My stomach's growling like a dog at a cat show, and I'm dying for something good to eat—some nice modern processed foods with artificial colors and additives."

"Okay. But be quiet so I can think." She tried a few unsuccessful rhymes in her head, but couldn't come up with anything good. "Darn! Should have brought my rhyming dictionary with me." After a moment she tried:

Girl with cat,
Time to scat,
Time to hurry
Home with furry.

"Ugh! That's the worst one yet!" Salem made a face, but crossed his paws anyway.

Again they both felt a jolt, as if they should be zapping through time and space. But when they opened their eyes and looked around, they were still in the same place.

Girl and cat,
Go home now—
The only rhyme I can think of is . . .
A big fat cow!

Somehow Sabrina and Salem weren't surprised to find themselves still standing in the same place. But Sabrina was taken aback at finding a big fat black-and-white cow standing next to them, chewing its cud.

"Ah, fair maiden, I'll trade you some magic beans for that fine cow," a man with a knapsack over his shoulder called out to her.

"Uh, I don't think so," Sabrina said quickly. "She's not for sale."

The man shrugged and hurried on. "Hey, Jack, hold up!" he called as he hurried to the other side of the marketplace.

"This is getting weird," Sabrina muttered as she sent the cow back to where it came from. "See, now, that spell worked!" she told Salem. "Why won't the others? Why can't I send *us* back to where *we* came from?"

"Beats me," Salem said, looking around. "But if you don't mind, I think I'll run and get a little snack while you figure things out."

"Salem, wait—"

But the hungry black cat had dashed off behind one of the food stalls to search for some tasty scraps.

Sabrina sighed and headed after him, keeping an eye out for Arthur the knight. He was awfully nice, and very cute, and normally she might like being put on a pedestal, but now she just wanted to get home. She had a lot of work to finish before classes on Monday.

Suddenly, across the center of the village, she spotted two familiar heads among the crowd.

Aunt Zelda and Aunt Hilda—she was sure of it!

They must have gotten out of their meeting with the Witches' Council earlier than they expected and come looking for me, she thought.

But then she noticed that they were dressed in period costumes, too. *They must be planning to spend the day here with me! How nice of them to come join me,* Sabrina thought. *They probably want to help me with my paper.*

She ran across the village square, tripping a little on her skirts in her eagerness to reach them.

"Aunt Zelda, Aunt Hilda!" she called out as she grew closer.

The two familiar figures turned around—

And Sabrina cried out in surprise!

It was her two aunts, all right. But they weren't six-hundred-year-old grown-ups.

They were teenagers!

And they looked at Sabrina as if they'd never seen her before in their lives.

Chapter 4

"Aunt Hilda!" Sabrina cried. "Aunt Zelda! It's me—Sabrina!"

She tried to shove her way through the crowded marketplace, but a minstrel singing about courtly love had drawn quite a crowd, and trying to get to her aunts was like trying to walk through waist-deep water. By the time she made her way to the other side of the crowd, the two girls had disappeared.

Sabrina looked around frantically, wondering where—and why—they'd gone. Hadn't they seen her? Hadn't they recognized her? If they had, why would they run off?

And why had they come to the Faire as young girls? Had something happened to them at the Witches' Council? Were they being punished for something? Or had someone cast some kind of bizarre spell on them to send them back in time?

Sabrina's head swam with all the questions. She had to sit down and think, somewhere away from the crowd.

Stumbling through the streets, she finally escaped down a worn path that led off into the woods. She didn't slow down until she was quite a way from the noise of the marketplace. At last she stopped and leaned against a tree, gasping for breath, trying to make sense out of what had gone wrong with her simple trip to this strange Medieval Faire.

And suddenly she felt hands around her neck.

She started to scream, but rough hands covered her mouth and dragged her into the woods.

She glanced around frantically at the handful of men who had grabbed her. They were dressed like all the other actors at the Faire.

But she could tell immediately that these men weren't playing games.

Their clothes were ragged and reeked of stale sweat. They grinned at her through rows of snaggleteeth that had never seen a modern dentist. Something in the way they spoke sounded rough and foreign, even though the words they used were English.

If I could just get my hands free, she thought . . . *Gotta think of a spell. . . .*

Then one of the men tried to yank her emerald necklace from her throat.

Now she understood what was going on. They were trying to steal her necklace. *Guess they don't pay these guys much.*

"Mm nhmm rmmml!" she tried to tell them. *It's not real!*

Before she could squirm free, she heard hoof beats pounding down the forest path.

She glanced up and nearly cheered—it was Arthur, her knight in shining armor, coming to her rescue!

Sabrina's head whirled. Was this whole thing part of the act, part of the play, part of the Faire?

She was terrified. Surely they wouldn't take the game this far. . . .

Then Arthur's mighty sword flashed in the sunlight, and the men scattered. The man holding her cried out in pain, and when she turned around, she saw red on the man's face.

Something tells me that's not ketchup, she thought.

And somehow she knew that this wasn't a

play. Right before she passed out in Arthur's arms, something in his eyes convinced her . . .

This was not a Medieval Faire outside of Westbridge, Massachusetts.

Somehow—she had no idea how—Sabrina had gone back in time to the *real* Middle Ages.

Chapter 5

"Sabrina . . . Sabrina, wake up!"

Sabrina stirred but didn't open her eyes. She'd been dreaming, dreaming she was being rescued from thieves by a handsome knight in shining armor, but now it was time to wake up. Time to open her eyes and say good-bye to the dream. . . .

She opened her eyes.

Arthur, her knight in shining armor, gazed down at her with his dazzling blue eyes. "Fair Sabrina, can you hear me? Are you all right?"

Sabrina closed her eyes again. Okay, time to wake up from the dream, Take Two. She stretched, took a deep breath, and opened her eyes again.

"How are you feeling?" Arthur asked.

"Why won't you go away?" Sabrina cried as she sat up.

Arthur looked hurt. "Go away?"

"You're in my dream and it's time for me to wake up now."

A jubilant smile spread across Arthur's handsome features. "Jubilation! The lady dreams of me!"

Sabrina cringed—not exactly the point she was trying to get across. But she'd have to face facts. Arthur wasn't a dream brought on by pigeon pie. He was real—and she was really confused.

"What year is this?" she asked him.

"What year?" He laughed, as if she meant to tease him. "Why, it is the year of our Lord fourteen hundred and eighty-seven."

"Okay, here come those champagne bubbles again," she muttered as she felt like fainting again.

But Arthur cradled her in his strong arms till her dizziness passed. "Those men . . . ?" she asked.

Arthur spat on the ground. "Gone, my fair lady. I only regret I was unable to skewer a few in your honor—"

"Uh—no problem," Sabrina insisted. "I'm just glad you came along and scared them off when you did." She held her hand to her throat, then gasped. "Oh, no! Where—"

"Looking for this?" Arthur held up Aunt Zelda's necklace, and its emerald sparkled in the afternoon sunlight slanting through the trees.

"Yes! Oh, thank you, Arthur!" She took the necklace into her hands and studied the jewel. She'd assumed it was fake, but could it be real? She decided to slip it back into the secret pocket on her sleeve, just in case.

"A wise move," Arthur said as he watched her.

Sabrina smiled as he helped her to her feet. "And I guess I should thank you for saving me. I don't know what I'd have done if you hadn't come by right when you did."

Instead of smiling in gratitude, Arthur scowled. "Of all the stupid, idiotic things . . . Didn't I tell you it wasn't safe to wander around alone unprotected? See where your pigheadedness almost got you?"

"What?"

"Just wait till your father hears what happened. He'll have my head and have you whipped!"

"My father's away on business," she informed him, although she didn't mention he was doing diplomatic service in another realm.

"Your husband then."

"I'm not married!"

Arthur seemed delighted at this news, although he answered, "And it's no wonder you're an old maid—the way you behave!"

Sabrina started to protest, then realized it was

pointless to argue women's lib with a fifteenth-century knight who was pledged to give his life if need be to protect a woman's honor. *I'll have to break the news to him slowly,* she decided. *Meanwhile, I've got to figure out what I'm doing here—and how to get home.*

"So, to whom are you entrusted?" Arthur asked her.

"Um, I guess you mean my aunts. I live with them." Then an idea occurred to her. "In fact, I thought I saw them in the marketplace. That's why I ran into the forest—I was looking for them. Could you—I mean, do you have time to help me find them?"

Arthur clanked as he bowed low before her. "I will make it my quest—I shall not rest until I reunite you with your aunts."

"Great! Thanks." She smiled at him. "I guess this means I'm getting back on your horse."

"Allow me to help you up."

As they rode through the marketplace, Sabrina spotted Salem lying in the sun next to the fishmonger's stall. "My cat!" Sabrina cried, pointing. "Salem, over here! Salem!"

Salem opened one eye, then jumped to his feet. Arthur slowed his horse so that Sabrina could reach down, and Salem leaped into her arms. "Salem, I've been worried about you."

Then she whispered into his ear, "You'll never guess what year it is! Fourteen eighty-seven."

"I know," Salem whispered back.

"You do? Then why aren't you worried?"

"Because," Salem whispered, "fourteen eighty-seven was a very good year for me."

"Whispering to your cat again?" Arthur said behind her. "Perhaps one day you'll whisper your secrets in my ear."

Uh-oh. Arthur was moving pretty fast here— and she didn't want to break his heart when she had to zap back to the twenty-first century. Even though those eyes of his were incredibly blue. . . .

Sabrina couldn't wait to get wherever it was they were going, especially since Salem kept squirming in her lap. But she gasped in surprise when they rode up to a huge castle surrounded by a stone wall. As Arthur pulled his horse to a halt, the drawbridge slowly creaked down. "Where are we going?" she asked Arthur. "Who lives here?"

"The Earl of Kensington, the lord of this castle and all the lands you see around here. It is he that I serve and . . . well, I'm fairly new at this," he confided. "So I hope you won't say anything about how I lost you in the marketplace that first time. It wouldn't look good for me."

"Oh, that wasn't your fault," Sabrina assured

him. "I'm known for disappearing at a moment's notice." She had to cough to cover up Salem's chuckle.

"It is kind of you to say so," Arthur said as they cantered across the drawbridge. "But I failed you and allowed you to fall prey to that band of ruthless thieves." He tucked a finger beneath her chin and turned her face toward his. "But I swear on all that is holy, I shall never fail you again, milady."

Okay, don't look at the blue eyes, Sabrina warned herself. *Don't look into the . . .*

Too late . . . and for the moment, she allowed herself to enjoy riding into a castle in the arms of a handsome knight. Heck, who knew how soon she'd get the chance again?

Once inside the castle walls, Arthur helped Sabrina down, then called for some men to take his horse to the stables. Then he turned to Sabrina. "You must be tired, milady. I shall show you to a guest room, where you can rest and recuperate."

"Thank you," Sabrina said, realizing she was indeed tired. She'd rest, wash up, then think about what to do. Maybe she'd try her magic again and see if it was working. And if that didn't work, she'd begin her search for Aunt Zelda and Aunt Hilda. They'd know what to do.

Once inside the castle, Arthur turned Sabrina

over to a lady's maid. "This is Gwendolyn," he introduced her. "She will see to your needs while you're here."

"Well, thanks," Sabrina said, "but I don't really need anyone to—"

"No arguments," Arthur said, laying his fingertips against Sabrina's lips. "You've had a horrifying day—a day no lady should have to endure. Go now with Gwendolyn. She'll take care of you."

Sabrina shrugged. Why fight it? "Cool," she said, then cringed when Gwendolyn instantly fetched her a shawl. *Gotta remember to keep a lid on the modern-day slang while I'm here,* Sabrina thought as she followed Gwendolyn to her room.

Sabrina's room was charming, if a little chilly, and the straw scattered about on the cold stone floor was a little strange to walk on at first. The maid built a roaring fire in the giant stone fireplace, then turned back the covers on the huge bed that stood nearby. Someone knocked, and Gwendolyn opened the door for two young boys, who entered carrying a large tub of steaming water. As soon as they left, Sabrina rolled back her sleeves and washed her hands and face with the warm water. *That felt good! People treat you so much better in the*

Middle Ages, she thought. Then she yawned and sat down on the bed.

"You should rest now, milady," Gwendolyn insisted. "May I help you off with your gown?"

"No, that's fine," Sabrina replied, especially since she was wearing modern underclothes beneath the gown. Besides, she didn't have time to sleep. She needed to begin her search for her aunts right away. "I don't want to sleep," she told Gwendolyn. "I'll just—*yawn!*—lie back for a few minutes and rest my eyes."

"As you wish, milady," Gwendolyn said with a small bow.

I could really get used to this, Sabrina thought as she lay back against the many pillows on the bed, although she felt a little guilty for letting Gwendolyn—a girl about her age—wait on her like a princess.

She felt Salem leap up onto the bed and curl up next to her feet.

And then she thought . . . nothing as she fell fast asleep.

When Sabrina awoke, she didn't know where she was at first, but as she looked around the room, it all came back to her.

She was in a castle during the Middle Ages, getting waited on by a knight and a lady's maid, and for some reason her magic wouldn't take her back home.

Gwendolyn was asleep on a pallet by the fire, and it was late at night. The castle was dark and quiet, and a full moon shone through the window of her room.

Then she heard a pebble bounce off the stone windowsill.

Sabrina tiptoed across the floor to the window and peered down into the night. Moonlight glinted off the armor of a dark-haired boy, who gazed up at her from the garden below as if she were a vision conjured from his imagination.

"Sabrina!" Arthur called up to her, smiling broadly. "How fare thee?"

"I fare fine," she called back down. "I mean, I'm good. Terrific. Couldn't be better." She couldn't help but admire the romantic image Arthur made standing beneath her window in the moonlight with his thick dark hair tumbling into his eyes. And the way she felt, standing here in her aunt's velvet gown . . . well, it was like living in the middle of a fairy tale. A fairy tale that couldn't last, but one that she let herself enjoy for the moment.

"It must be late," Sabrina called down to Arthur. "What are you doing down there?"

"I had to see your lovely face one more

time," he called to her. "And I wanted to tell you good-bye."

"Good-bye?" Sabrina exclaimed, then glanced at Gwendolyn, to make sure she hadn't woken her. "But, Arthur, where are you going?"

"I went to the chapel and pledged myself to a quest," he announced.

"A quest? What kind of quest?"

"A quest to win your favor," he declared.

Sabrina couldn't deny that her heart jumped a beat at his words. "What are you going to do?" she asked.

"I'm off to slay a dragon," Arthur revealed. "A traveling minstrel reported to the earl tonight that a dragon has been sighted just north of here, terrorizing some of Lord Kensington's people and setting fire to the forest. I shall slay him in your name . . . and hope for a small crumb of affection from you in return."

"But, Arthur—"

"Nay, do not say a thing," Arthur called up. "I know I am not worthy of your attentions. But perhaps when I return with the head of this dragon, I shall turn your heart my way."

"But, no—Arthur, what I was going to say was . . ." She hated to embarrass him, but the truth had to be said. "There is no such thing as a dragon!"

Arthur beamed in the moonlight. "Ah, the fair lady fears for my safety and tries to dissuade me from my dangerous journey! Dare I hope she begins to favor me? I shall carry this morsel of encouragement in my heart to inspire my courage as I face the fiery breath of my enemy!"

"No, Arthur, wait! I need you here—"

"She needs me!" Arthur announced to the stars as he leaped onto his horse. "Fear not, fair Sabrina! For I shall return to your arms victorious before the moon wanes!"

"Arthur, wait! No!" Her heart sank as she watched him gallop off in the moonlight. He was her champion, and she needed his help to figure out how to get out of this place and back home, where she belonged.

"Guess he couldn't hear you through all that armor," Salem commented as he leaped to the windowsill. Then he giggled and added, "I never knew you were into heavy metal, Sabrina."

Sabrina scowled at her cat. "You're not funny, and if you don't behave, I'll leave you here to rot when I go home."

"So?" Salem sniffed. "I've been here before. And this time I'm only a cat. Nothing to do but sleep all day on a fat feather bed."

Sabrina folded her arms and smiled. "So

you're ready to give up air-conditioning, voice mail, canned sardines, and your stock portfolio?"

All the hair stood up on Salem's back. "Sabrina, don't leave me here. I beg of you!"

"Calm down, Salem. I won't leave you. But if I don't get some help soon, I might be staying here myself—indefinitely."

Salem glanced at Gwendolyn, who appeared to be snoring gently by the fire. "So, have you tried your magic again?"

"Not yet. Perhaps I should." She stepped away from the window, composing a new spell. "How's this?"

Girl in red,
Black-haired kitty,
Say ciao to the castle
And go home to the city.

"Ooh, I like that one!" Salem exclaimed. He closed his eyes, waiting for the spell to work.

They felt a familiar jolt, but otherwise, nothing seemed to happen.

"I don't get it," Sabrina said, her shoes rustling on the rushes as she paced the room. "It's as if the magic starts to work, but then something interferes with it."

"Try one more time," Salem begged.

Sabrina sighed and folded her arms across her chest. Then she began to jump up and down, shouting:

I wanna go home!
I wanna go home!
I summon all my magic, 'cause—
I WANNA GO HOME!

Sabrina felt a cosmic hiccup run through her body and thought she was on her way at last. She even felt her feet rise from the floor—

But a second later she landed right where she had begun.

"We're doomed!" Salem wailed as he jumped on the bed and buried his way beneath the covers.

Sabrina felt like joining him, but this was no time to give in to her fears. *I'm relatively smart. I'm resourceful. I can figure this out,* she told herself.

Maybe it's like the computer at home, she thought. *Sometimes if the computer freezes up, you just have to shut down and restart.*

Sabrina took a deep breath and imagined herself shutting down. Then she started all over again by trying some simple magic.

She pointed at a mug of cider that Gwendolyn had left on the table by her bed in case she became thirsty in the night. She wriggled her finger and tried to levitate it.

"Yes!" Sabrina cried as the mug rose and hovered a foot off the table. "I haven't lost all my magic!"

Next she tried something a little harder. She made Salem rise in the air.

Floating in the air, Salem poked his head out from under the covers. "Sabrina! That's not funny! Put me down!" But then his eyes popped open. "Hey! You're doing magic! You're fixed! Quick—put me down and try a home spell again."

Sabrina quickly lowered Salem to the bed, then tried a new spell to take them home.

Oh, powers of magic,
I beg of you please,
Send me back home
With the greatest of ease.

Again the feeling of transition, but when it passed, they were still in the castle bedroom.

"I just don't get it," Sabrina complained. "I've just got to find Aunt Zelda and Aunt Hilda. Otherwise I might never get out of here."

"Sabrina!" Salem said suddenly.

"What?"

"Where's Gwendolyn?"

"Right over—" She pointed to the girl's bed by the fire, but it was empty.

Sabrina whirled around. "She's gone! But when did she leave?"

"She never made a sound," Salem said gravely. "Do you think she heard us? Do you think she saw you do your magic before she slipped out?"

Suddenly the bedroom door slammed open and two guards rushed in to grab Sabrina by the arms.

"Yes," Sabrina replied weakly as the guards dragged her from the room.

Chapter 6

"They didn't even give you a fair trial!" Salem complained.

The two guards had wasted no time in dragging her to the dungeon and throwing her into a dark, dank cell in the bowels of the castle. "They didn't give me any kind of trial. Guess they haven't passed that law yet, huh?" Sabrina grasped the cold bars of the cell door and yanked on them, even though she knew they'd probably locked her in and thrown away the key.

"If only I had a cell phone . . ." Salem wailed as he paced in front of her cell. "I need to call you a lawyer!"

"Give it up, Salem," Sabrina counseled him. "We've been busted, big time. No use trying to reason with these guys, you should know that. We've gotta play by their rules."

Salem stopped and stared up at her as if she were insane. "Sabrina! I don't think you understand. This is the Middle Ages, sweetheart. They don't like witches here. Witches give them the heebie-jeebies. They try to get rid of them—and I don't even want to tell you how."

"I know, Salem, but you're not going to charm your way out of this one. We've got to escape!"

"You cannot," said a voice from an inky black corner of the cell.

Sabrina jumped back against the door. "Hello? Is someone there?"

A shape in the darkness rose and walked into the dim light cast by a lone sputtering candle stuck into a hole in the wall.

A tall handsome man appeared before Sabrina. Above his pure white beard, his eyes sparkled in a way that seemed to defy anyone to guess his age. He seemed old and wise, and yet young and full of energy all at the same time. "Allow me to introduce myself. My name is Marlin. I was a wizard under the protection of Lord Kensington, and an apprentice of the great Merlin."

"Merlin? Wow—I've read about him," Sabrina said. "But I was never sure if he was real or just a legend."

"Oh, he was definitely real," Marlin said. "A true genius. A bit ahead of his time, really."

"My name is Sabrina, and this is my cat, Salem."

"Ah, yes. The talking cat. Most interesting."

Uh-oh. He heard! How am I going to explain that? But then, Marlin didn't seem too upset about it. "A talking cat doesn't, well, freak you out?"

Marlin smiled. "I am a man who takes the world as it comes, studies it, then records the facts while trying to understand its mysteries. There are many strange things in the world that can be explained rationally if only we work hard enough to figure them out. If I see a cat that talks, I don't think, 'Cats don't talk.' I think, 'Why does this cat talk, and how does he do it?' Besides, I once had a cat I was sure could talk, but I could never get him to speak up."

Sabrina laughed. "My Aunt Zelda is a scientist, too. She teaches at the college I go to."

"Really? A woman who has devoted her life to science? Extraordinary! This is a woman I'd love to meet."

"And I wish I could introduce you," Sabrina said with a sigh. "So why are you in here?"

"Well, they were happy enough with my little feats of magic when I entertained them, and when I worked on experiments to turn various metals into gold that would replenish the castle's coffers," he explained. "But when I began to do serious experiments on the real world, based on knowledge and science—things they feared—" He shrugged. "Then they began to call me a warlock."

Sabrina nodded. "That's what I'm in here for, too. Being a witch."

"Really?" Marlin smiled eagerly. "So you want to be a scientist like your aunt, hmm? So what kind of research were you doing?"

Sabrina wasn't sure what to say, so she just said, "Oh . . . I guess you could call it time travel."

"Ah! Fascinating! I've been studying the scientific possibilities myself. Too bad we can't figure it out while we're in here—it would definitely come in handy."

"I'll say." Sabrina went to the door of the cell and peered through the bars into the dark corridor. Water dripped from the ceiling, echoing down the long empty halls. She tried not to think about the rat she thought she saw skitter across the stones. "So how long do you think they'll keep us prisoner down here?"

"Oh, not long. Not long at all. In fact"—he glanced through the bars as if expecting company—"they should be coming for us soon."

"Really? Cool! I can't wait to get out."

"Don't hurry time, young one, for it passes quickly enough on its own," Marlin warned her. "And when we leave this place, it most definitely will not be cool."

"Really? Why not?"

"Because, my dear, when they come for us, it won't be to set us free, I'm afraid."

Sabrina gulped. "It w-won't?"

Marlin shook his head. "It will be to burn us at the stake for being witches."

Chapter 7

"Say that again?" Sabrina gasped. "No, wait—don't repeat it. Don't even think it!"

Marlin laid a comforting hand on her shoulder, but shrugged philosophically. "I'm sorry, child. It's what they do with witches in these parts. A bit ignorant and backward, I agree. But then, the masses always have trouble with new ideas. But put your mind at ease, my dear. I have a potion for when the time comes . . . something to render us unconscious so that we don't feel the pain."

"Uh, thanks a whole lot, I appreciate that—really I do," Sabrina sputtered. "But if you don't mind—I think I'd really like to consider the alternatives here. I'm too young to be burned at the stake! And besides, I borrowed this dress from

Aunt Zelda and I promised I'd get it back to her without scorch marks."

Marlin's hearty laughter echoed against the cold stone walls. "I like your spunk, child. You would have made a wonderful apprentice."

"Maybe I still will." Sabrina grabbed the bars and called down to her cat. "Salem! There's got to be a way out of here! Quick! Go snoop around. See what you can find out about the guards."

"Do I have to?" Salem whined.

"Not if you'd rather be the main course at a major barbecue," she commented.

Salem's tail shot up in the air. "Hey! I'm no witch! I'm just a warlock who's been stripped of all his powers! Surely they wouldn't . . ."

Sabrina glared at him.

"I'll see what I can do."

Sabrina watched Salem dart off through the shadows, up the cold, moldy stairs. And she couldn't help but wonder . . . *Will I ever see him again?*

"So tell me," Marlin asked, "what sciences do you know?"

"Well, I took chemistry, biology, and earth sciences in school. And I took a mini astronomy course at summer camp one year. And . . ." She watched closely for his reaction. "I can do a little bit of magic here and there."

"Excellent!" Marlin said, nodding and stroking his beard. "Magic is a little bit science, and science is a little bit magic, I always say."

Aunt Zelda would love this guy, Sabrina thought.

A few minutes later footsteps rang out on the stone steps.

"Someone's coming!" Sabrina whispered as she grabbed Marlin's hand. Despite his philosophical attitude, she felt his cold hand tremble a little in hers.

"Sounds like two sets of footsteps," Marlin whispered.

Maybe I can stall them with a little magic, Sabrina thought. *If I can get anything to work . . .*

Sabrina braced herself, but when the two figures moved into the faint candlelight, she gasped in surprise.

It was Aunt Zelda and Aunt Hilda!

The teenage Zelda and Hilda.

"Woo-hoo!" Sabrina shouted, then said to the wizard, "Don't worry, Marlin. We are so out of here!"

"Sabrina," Salem called to her from the stairs. "I think you ought to know—"

But Sabrina was too excited to listen. "Aunt Zelda, Aunt Hilda—I'm so glad you're here! This is my friend Marlin—he's sort of one of us. Get us out of here—quick!"

Zelda and Hilda stared at her curiously.

"How do you know our names?" Zelda asked.

"Huh?" Sabrina's gaze darted between the two girls. "Because I'm Sabrina! I know you! You're my . . ." Her voice trailed off as she took in the expressions on the two young witches' faces. They looked as if they had no idea who Sabrina was!

"Salem—"

"I tried to tell you," Salem said as he squeezed through the bars and leaped into her arms. His voice dropped to a whisper, "They don't know us. This Zelda and Hilda live here, now, in this time. You haven't even been born yet, so they can't possibly know you. And I haven't been turned into a cat yet, so they don't know me, either."

So that explained everything—including her aunts' behavior in the marketplace the day before. They hadn't recognized her because they didn't know her. These weren't her aunts come back in time to find her. She had just met her aunts as young girls! "Whoa . . ." was all she could say.

"Your cat tells us you're one of us," young Zelda said in a low voice.

"I . . . yes. I am."

"I told you so," Hilda fussed at her sister. "I knew the minute I saw her in the marketplace. But you wouldn't listen—"

"Hush!" Zelda told her younger sister. "We've got more important things to do than listen to you babble."

"You're not the boss of me!" Hilda shot back. "Just because you're older doesn't mean you can—"

"Hilda! Zelda!"

The girls stopped bickering and stared at Sabrina.

"Sorry to interrupt," Sabrina said, convinced beyond a doubt now that these were really her aunts. "But we need to hurry. Marlin here thinks we don't have much time before they come for us."

Hilda folded her arms and squinted at Sabrina. "Hold your steeds, Blondie. If you're one of us, how come you can't use your magic to get out of here?"

"Hilda, don't be rude!" Zelda admonished.

"Well, it's a legitimate question, isn't it?"

Zelda looked at Sabrina apologetically, but answered, "She does have a point, Sabrina."

"I've tried a dozen spells to send me and my cat home," Sabrina explained. "But they don't work. Each time I feel something happening, as if the magic had worked, but it never sends me home. I just wind up right here again."

Zelda laid a finger on her cheek—a gesture

Sabrina had seen Aunt Zelda use thousands of times when she was pondering a problem. "Strange . . ."

"Prove it," Hilda blurted out.

"What?"

"Prove you're a witch. If you can't do big magic, do something small."

"Hilda!" Zelda exclaimed. "For goodness' sake. Where are your manners?"

"Manners?" Hilda's eyes flashed. "I never met this girl before in my life. How do we know she's not just setting us up? Trying to prove that *we're* witches?"

Zelda looked at Sabrina apologetically. "Amazingly, again, she does have a point."

"I don't mind a little demonstration," Sabrina answered. She ran a hand through her hair and tried to think. "I just hope this works. . . ."

She thought a moment, then tried:

Dear Mr. Marlin,
I enjoyed our chat.
I hope you don't mind
If I turn you into a cat.

Zelda winced. "A few too many syllables in that last line . . ."

"Now who's being rude?" Hilda demanded.

But they both gasped in delight when Marlin the wizard turned into an elegant white cat.

"A playmate!" Salem exclaimed.

"Nicely done," Zelda said with a smile.

"Oooh! He's adorable," Hilda squealed as she reached through the bars and scooped Marlin the cat into her arms. "Can I have him?"

"I don't think so," Sabrina said.

"Absolutely not," Zelda agreed. "Besides, you know father's allergic."

Sabrina decided not to risk leaving Marlin in his altered state, just in case her magic went on the blink again, so she quickly uttered another spell:

Dear Mr. Marlin,
Hope you had fun.
But it's time to change back—
Our experiment's done.

Sparkles flew from Sabrina's fingertip as she changed the white cat back into a wizard.

"Ooof!" Hilda collapsed beneath the weight of the wizard in her arms.

"Oops! Sorry about that!" Sabrina said.

"Fascinating!" Marlin cried as he stared at his hands that for a few minutes had been furry white paws.

"Excellent!" Zelda cried, clapping her hands.

"I'm very impressed, Sabrina." But then her eyes clouded over with concern. "So why doesn't all your magic work?"

Sabrina shrugged. "I don't know. But maybe if I can get out of here, I can figure that out. Can you help us?"

"Of course we will," Zelda replied. "We witches have to stick together."

"And what about Marlin?" Sabrina asked. "He's been very kind to me."

Hilda narrowed her eyes at him. "You're not gonna rat on us once you're out, are you?"

"Heavens, no!" Marlin cried. "Turn you over to the unenlightened mob? I'd like to study with you. I think we have a lot in common—and a lot we can share with one another."

"Fine," Zelda said. "Stand back then. We're all going for a little ride." Zelda whispered an incantation, waved her arms in the air . . .

"Salem, quick!" Sabrina shouted.

The quick cat leaped into her arms just as footsteps rang out in the corridor.

The guards!

Just as—

Poof!

Sabrina felt herself swept away by Zelda's spell.

Chapter 8

"I remember this place!" Salem exclaimed as they all landed inside Zelda and Hilda's home, in the room the girls used to study and practice their magic.

"You do?" Hilda asked suspiciously. "Since when?"

Sabrina gave Salem a hard look.

"Oh, uh, we walked by once when Sabrina took me on a walk," Salem fibbed. Then he whispered in Sabrina's ear: "I knew them when they lived here. Does that mean I exist in this time in my human form of Salem Saberhagen, the warlock? What happens if I meet myself?"

"Shh," Sabrina whispered back. "That's too complicated even to think about right now! Let's just worry about getting ourselves home."

"Marvelous laboratory," Marlin said as he walked around the room, examining the girls' many jars of potions, crystals, and bottles of magic ingredients.

"Don't touch anything," Hilda warned him.

"Hilda!" Zelda exclaimed. "That's no way to talk to our guests."

"Well, what if he breaks something?" Hilda replied. "Or spills some tincture of gecko into some half-finished experiment of yours and turns us all into ogres or something? This is not a hands-on discovery museum, you know."

"Hilda, Mr. Marlin is a scientist. I'm sure he'll be very careful, won't you, Mr. Marlin?"

"Of course!" Marlin replied.

Sabrina noticed that Marlin and Aunt Zelda held each other's gaze just a little longer than one might expect. *Why, I think they quite admire each other,* Sabrina thought. *Too bad they couldn't know each other in Westbridge, in the future. . . .*

"Now, then," Zelda announced, blushing a little as she turned back to the matter at hand. "Let's get to work. You're trying to get home, right, Sabrina?" She opened a huge black book of spells. Sabrina gasped when she realized it was the same one her aunts had given her back in Westbridge, on her sixteenth birthday, when they first revealed to her that she was a witch.

"Let's start at the beginning," Zelda suggested. "What village are you from?"

"Well, it's a little more complicated than that," Sabrina tried to explain. "You see, I don't live around here anywhere."

"Ah, you're from a foreign country, then," Zelda said, flipping to another section in the book.

"Sort of, only much farther than that. I'm from a town called Westbridge, in a country that hasn't even been created yet."

Everyone looked at her.

Sabrina decided not to go into the part about Hilda and Zelda being her aunts. Instead, she simply told them, "You see, Salem and I—we're from the future."

Hilda, Zelda, and Marlin stared.

"Fascinating!" Marlin said at last, his eyes shining with excitement. "I had no idea when you said you were working on time travel that you'd actually done it! How on earth did you accomplish it?"

"I don't know exactly," Sabrina explained. "That's part of the problem. I was in a sticky situation back home. I uttered a spell—and zap! I found myself here. And no matter how hard I try,

I can't seem to reverse the magic and send myself home."

Zelda sighed. "This is going to be a tough one. Father has spoken to us of traveling through space and time. But we haven't gotten to that chapter yet in our lessons."

Marlin joined her in front of the book of magic. "Perhaps if we both put our heads together, we can discover the mystery."

Zelda smiled up into his eyes as their hands touched on the pages of the book.

"Can we get on with it, please?" Hilda groused. She glanced at Sabrina and scowled. "I don't get it. Zelda gets all the smart guys. I always wind up with the losers. So tell me, what's up with that?"

Sabrina smothered a smile. It was the same complaint Hilda still had back home in the future.

After an hour or so of research, experiments, debates, and recipe testing, Zelda, Hilda, and Marlin came up with a potion that they hoped would restore Sabrina's magic. But they needed one ingredient that Sabrina's young aunts didn't have on their shelves.

A dragon's eye.

"Ewww, sounds gross!" Salem commented from his spot in the corner, where he'd been playing cat and mouse with a mouse.

"I know," Zelda said.

"But we don't have one anyway," Hilda said. "What are you going to do?"

Sabrina smiled. "Don't worry. Hilda, Zelda, I think it's time I looked up an old friend. But I might need to borrow some of your magic."

"My turn!" Hilda insisted, rubbing her hands together. "So, where do you want to go?"

Chapter 9

Splash!

"Help! I'm drowning!" Salem cried.

Sabrina, Salem, Zelda, Hilda, and Marlin found themselves sprawled in a huge vat of mead in the basement of the Earl of Kensington's castle.

"Thanks a lot, Hilda!" Zelda sputtered as she shoved her wet blond hair out of her face.

"Okay, okay, so my locator spell needs a little work," Hilda said with a frown. "I only learned it last month."

Sabrina climbed out of the vat and scooped a flailing Salem out of the brew.

"Don't worry," Hilda assured them. "I won't mess it up this time."

"That's for certain," Aunt Zelda said. "Because you're not going to try it again. I'll take care of it."

"That's not fair!" Hilda said. "It's my turn to do some magic."

"But I'm older," Zelda insisted. "I've been practicing longer than you."

"Ladies, ladies, this is not a contest," Marlin interrupted as he squeezed the liquid from his beard.

Hilda scowled, but stepped aside to let her sister have a go.

First Zelda used her magic to rinse them with mountain spring water, then zapped them all dry.

"Show-off," Hilda muttered.

Then Zelda recited an incantation so quietly Sabrina could barely hear.

As she leaned forward to listen, she felt all her atoms tingle like a freshly opened can of diet soda . . .

And instantly they were on a hillside outside the village.

"Oooh," Salem said. "That was tingly! Can we do it again?"

"No time for that now," Sabrina said as she looked around. Had Zelda done it? Had she found the one person Sabrina was looking for and delivered them to him?

A flash of lightning caught her eye, and she studied the hills above them. There, near the top of the highest hill, she saw another flash of lightning—only it wasn't lightning. It flared like a plume of fire in some magic act.

"The dragon," Sabrina breathed.

"Um, I think I'll just stand over here behind this nice big rock and . . . um, supervise," Salem said.

Sabrina frantically searched the hillside. *Where is . . .?*

And then she spotted him—the lone brave figure standing in the glare of that ferocious fire like a tiny action figure before the flames of a huge incinerator.

Her knight in shining armor.

Her heart did a funny little somersault. Somehow she'd developed an affection for the foolish young knight. And then she jumped when flames seemed to engulf him.

"Arthur!" she shouted. "Arthur!" *He's going to be flame-broiled by a dragon, and it's all my fault! He ought to be home playing basketball . . . or whatever it is they play here.*

I've got to save him!

"Sabrina, wait!" Marlin shouted.

But Sabrina ignored him, hiked up her skirts, and ran.

"Arthur!" she shouted. "Arthur!"

At last he heard her and whirled around. At first he looked delighted to see her, but then his face twisted into an expression of horror. "Sabrina!" he shouted. "What are you doing here? This is no place for a lady!"

"I'm not a lady!" she cried, shocking him even further. "I mean, I am," she added as she reached him and took his hands in hers. "But not the kind who's content to sit around the castle all day embroidering or having her hair braided. I know you won't understand what I'm going to tell you," she rushed on, "but I'm from the future, Arthur. From a time and place where girls aren't weaklings sitting around on pedestals content with simply being admired. We can take care of ourselves."

"But, Sabrina," Arthur said, his eyes troubled and confused. "I—I like you! I *want* to take care of you. That's what knights in shining armor are supposed to do. At least, that's what they taught me in knight school."

"I know," Sabrina said. "But I promise you, I can take care of myself."

Arthur's sword sagged to the ground. "Then you don't need me for anything."

Oh! Sabrina couldn't stand it—Arthur looked just like a sad little puppy. "But I do need you, Arthur." She explained to him their quest to find a dragon's eye. And then she squeezed his hand. "Think we can do it—together?"

Hope flared in Arthur's eyes. "You're a strange girl, Sabrina, but . . . I kind of like that."

Sabrina grinned. "Come on, then. Let's go slay us a dragon."

What a battle ensued! The dragon was firmly entrenched in his hillside lair, and any attempt to approach him prompted another blast of angry, acrid fire.

This is getting us nowhere, Sabrina thought, then glanced at Arthur. *He looks awful!* Sabrina was hot enough in her long velvet gown, but Arthur must be roasting inside all that metal.

"Arthur, listen. I've got an idea. You stay here and wave your sword around, you know, distract the beast while I sneak around the back way."

"No, Sabrina, I cannot allow it—"

"Don't even go there," Sabrina warned him with a grin. "I'll be fine. I've been in worse scrapes than this, I promise." *You wouldn't believe,* she added to herself.

Arthur sighed and wiped the sweat from his brow. "Okay . . . but this is all so different and confusing."

"Different and confusing can be good," Sabrina told him. "It means we're thinking. And, Arthur? Why don't you take off some of that hot armor. You look miserable!"

"But then I won't be—"

"A knight in shining armor," Sabrina chimed in along with him. "It's more a concept than a literal way to dress."

"Do you think so?"

"Definitely. The armor's just a prop. I think you'll do just great as plain old Arthur."

Arthur just stared at her a moment with those intense blue eyes of his, as if he were trying to see right into her mind. "No one's ever said anything like that to me before, milady."

"I think we're past all that 'milady' stuff. It's nice, but, well, I'm a pretty ordinary girl, so 'Sabrina' will do just fine."

"Okay . . . Sabrina. But believe me, you're far from ordinary." He yanked off his heavy metal chest plate and tossed it to the ground, then grasped Sabrina by the hand. "Good luck, Sabrina."

"Good luck, Arthur." She held his hand a moment longer, then turned toward the hills . . .

And her first up-close-and-personal interview with a real live dragon.

"I sure could use a pair of jeans right now," Sabrina muttered as she climbed the hillside in Zelda's elegant velvet gown. That's what was so cool about the twenty-first century—a girl could dress up or dress down and still be a true lady.

And this lady's about to slay her a dragon.

Of course, it would be nice if she had an idea what she was actually going to do when she got there. Her best plan right now involved trying some kind of magic—and hoping that it worked.

There, up ahead! An opening in the hillside. *Might be the back entrance of the dragon's cave.*

But as she stepped forward, a twig cracked beneath her foot, and suddenly—

Sabrina stared straight into the emerald-green eyes of a living, fire-breathing dragon!

The huge scaly beast roared its greeting.

"I'm toast!" Sabrina squeaked as she closed her eyes and waited for the fiery blast.

☆

Chapter 10

☆

Nothing happened.

O-kay . . . I'm still here. What's going on?

She cautiously opened one eye to see what the big green guy was up to.

"*R-O-O-O-A-A-R-R-R!*"

"*Eeeeek!*" Sabrina shrieked and tumbled backward onto her bottom. And without thinking what she was saying, she shouted, "Stop that! Eat me alive—or burn me to a crisp. But don't just scare me. That's just plain mean and rude!"

Then she clapped her hand over her mouth. *Good one, Sabrina. Take one mean, ornery killer dragon—and insult him. That'll really get him mad!*

But never in a million centuries could she have predicted what happened next.

The dragon began to cry.

Big, fat salty tears rained down on Sabrina like . . . well, rain. Sabrina quickly scooted out from under the waterfall of hot tears and scrambled to her feet, watching in amazement as the dragon continued to cry his eyes out.

"Um, excuse me," Sabrina said at last, in a rather kind voice. "Are you all right?"

"Of course I'm not all right!" the dragon cried. "You—you hurt my feelings! Boo-hoo-hoo . . ."

Now I've seen everything, Sabrina thought with a shake of her head. "Yes, well, but you scared me."

The dragon tried to blink back his tears. "I'm sorry. . . . But you snuck up on me."

"But you were attacking my friend Arthur."

"Well, he attacked me first!"

"Hold it! Hold it right there." Sabrina jammed her fists on her hips and studied the pitifully sobbing monster. "Let me get this straight. The only reason you're being ornery and mean is because we're being mean to *you?*"

"Exactly!" the dragon exclaimed. "Finally—somebody who *understands* me! *Boo-hoo-hoo.*"

"Now, now, there's no need to cry now. I'm not going to hurt you." And Sabrina knew as she said it that it was true, regardless of the fact that she'd come here in search of a dragon's eye, the one last ingredient she needed for a potion that might send her home to her own time. This creature wasn't a monster at all, he was just big, and rather magnificent, actually—if a bit of a crybaby—and there was no way in the world she could bring herself to hurt him on purpose.

Sabrina cautiously stepped closer and patted the sobbing beast on the leg. "Tell me about it."

The dragon sniffled. "How would you like it if you were off in your own cave, minding your own business, and people kept coming on these huge quests to attack you—just so they could show off to their silly, fickle girlfriends!"

Sabrina was beginning to see the whole picture. "I guess that would make me pretty cranky, too," she admitted.

"But why do you hoard all this treasure? I mean, after all, what does a dragon need with gold and jewels?"

"I used to share," the dragon said with a pout. "But nobody ever says please anymore."

"Hey, I know what that's like!" She sat down on a big rock and sighed, trying to figure out what to do. The dragon laid his head on the ground, so his face was right in front of her. He really did have beautiful eyes, like giant green emeralds sparkling in sunlight.

"You're nice," the dragon said at last. "What's your name?"

"Sabrina."

The dragon smiled. "I like that name. My name's Charles."

"Really?"

"Um-hmm. Like it?"

Sabrina studied the huge green beast and smiled. "It suits you perfectly."

"Sabrina, why did you come here?" Charles asked softly.

Sabrina swallowed guiltily and tried to come up with a quick fib. But since this relationship was at a critical stage, she decided it was best to be honest. "Well, I'm not going to do what I came here to do anymore, but . . . well, we came to get a dragon's eye. I needed it for a spell so I could go home. But don't worry!" she added quickly. "I wouldn't hurt you now for the world!"

Then the dragon did something even more amazing.

He laughed out loud.

"What are you laughing at?" Sabrina asked in amazement.

"I know that spell," Charles said, still chuckling. "You silly witches! It doesn't mean to use a *real* dragon's eye! *Gross!* The spell calls for a dragon's eye *emerald!*"

"Really?" Sabrina exclaimed. "Hey, that's great!"

"Um, actually, it's not."

"I don't get it."

"Dragon's eye emeralds are extremely rare," Charles explained. "I used to have one in my treasure, but unfortunately I don't have it anymore," he admitted. "A couple of years ago I somehow got my foot stuck in a rocky cliff. By and by a warlock came along and quickly freed me. Other men would have run away in fear or, even worse, taken advantage of my situation and cut off my head for a trophy. In return for the warlock's kindness I offered him anything he wanted from my treasures. He chose the dragon's eye emerald. He said he was going to have it made into a necklace to give to his oldest daughter on her next birthday."

Sabrina gasped in astonishment. *It couldn't be . . . could it?* She reached into the secret pocket in the sleeve of Aunt Zelda's gown and pulled out the necklace . . . the necklace with the huge beautiful emerald. "Is this your dragon's eye?"

"That's it!" the dragon exclaimed in surprise. "I'd know it anywhere. Oh, my. It does make a lovely necklace." But then he cocked his head, puzzled. "But how did you come to possess it?"

"I borrowed this dress from the warlock's daughter," she said, pointing to her rather rumpled gown. "My aunt Zelda. And I found the necklace hidden in this pocket in the sleeve. I had no idea it was so special."

"And powerful, too," Charles told her.

"Powerful?" Sabrina dangled the emerald in front of her eyes and studied it. "What does it do?"

"It gives the owner the ability to wish herself home in an instant," the dragon explained. "No matter where she is."

Sabrina frowned as she studied this news. "But that doesn't make any sense. I kept trying to go home. I made up a dozen perfectly adequate spells. But even though I had the dragon's eye emerald in my possession, it never took me home. I always wound up in this same old village. . . ."

The dragon smiled. "Come now, Sabrina. I think you can figure that one out."

Sabrina thought. And then she smiled. "Ah, I get it. It gives the *owner* the ability to go to her home in an instant."

Charles nodded. "So whenever you said a spell, the emerald took you home—to the necklace's owner's home."

"Aunt Zelda's home when she owned the necklace was in the Middle Ages! Which is where I already was," Sabrina stated. "No wonder!"

She and the dragon had a good laugh. Then

she stood up. "Come on. I want you to meet my friends."

"Really?" the dragon said. He looked so happy, Sabrina was afraid he was going to start crying all over again. "Yeah, but don't cry, you might put out your flame."

Charles laughed. "It would take a lot more than that to put out this flame."

A few minutes later Sabrina stood at the mouth of the dragon's lair. "Hey, you guys!" she shouted down to her aunts, Marlin, Arthur, and Salem. "Hold your fire. You, too, Charles," she said over her shoulder. "There's somebody here I'd like you to meet."

Then she motioned for Charles the dragon to come out. As soon as the giant green monster revealed himself, Arthur freaked. "Sabrina! I'm coming! I'll save you!"

"Hold it, Arthur!" Sabrina shouted. "Put down your sword. We're all friends here."

And with that Sabrina introduced the knight and the dragon. It was quite an unusual sight.

"Sabrina," Arthur said, "I've never met anybody like you."

"Me, neither," said Charles.

"Too bad we don't have any marshmallows!" Salem remarked, coming out from his hiding place behind the rock.

"Who says we don't?" And with a blink of her eye, Sabrina conjured up a whole bagful.

"Your magic! It's working fine again," Marlin exclaimed.

"There was never anything wrong with it," Sabrina said. They all found sticks and Sabrina passed out the marshmallows. And as they all gathered around Charles's flame to toast marshmallows, Sabrina explained the whole story.

"So you see, this dress I'm wearing is really *your* dress," Sabrina told Zelda.

"I thought it looked like mine," Zelda replied. "But I didn't want to say anything. I was afraid it might sound rude. But, Sabrina, there's only one thing I don't understand. How did you come to have it?"

Sabrina gazed fondly at Zelda and Hilda. *Should I tell them? Are they ready to hear the truth?*

"You see, there's something I didn't tell you guys," Sabrina began. "Back home, in the future? Well, you're my aunts."

"You mean—"

"Your brother Ted is my dad," Sabrina explained.

"Oh! Ted is going to be so mad he's traveling in the Orient and missed you."

"That's okay," Sabrina said. "It's weird enough meeting your aunts before you're born."

Zelda and Hilda hugged her, but then Hilda frowned and gave Zelda a little punch. "You see? I *told* you I didn't take your necklace!" She turned to Sabrina. "For years she's been claiming that I stole her necklace—"

"I always said 'borrowed,' " Zelda insisted.

"And all along, you forgot that you'd put it in that secret pocket!" Hilda complained.

Oh, no, Sabrina thought. *Are they going to start fighting all over again?*

But Zelda was smiling. "I'm sorry, little sister. I should have known you were telling the truth."

Hilda sniffled. "I'm sorry, too, big sister. It's my fault. I usually *do* take your stuff!"

"That's okay," Zelda said as they hugged each other. "You can borrow any of my things any-time."

Suddenly it began to rain—big, fat dragon tears. "I love it when people make up!" Charles bawled.

"Stop!" Salem shouted. "You'll make the marshmallows soggy!"

Then the big, fat tears dried up as everybody laughed.

Chapter 11

Back in the Spellman sisters' workroom, everybody put their heads together to try to figure out how to send Sabrina and Salem home.

Everybody except Arthur. He didn't want her to go.

But Sabrina knew it was time. "Gotta go," she said.

Zelda and Marlin were poring over her books and experimenting with her potions.

"Now, I think," Zelda said, "we can use my dragon's eye emerald in this spell, but with these substitutions . . ." She added a pinch of this, and Marlin stirred in a pinch of that. "This should send you right home." She laid her hand on Sabrina's shoulder. "Ready?"

Sabrina looked around at Marlin the sorcerer-scientist. Charles the unbelievable dragon. And Arthur. The knight in shining armor who almost stole her heart.

And most of all her aunts, as young girls, about the same age as Sabrina.

"I don't want to say good-bye," she admitted with tears in her eyes.

Zelda smiled, wiser than her years. "We'll always be with you, in your heart."

Sabrina nodded, too choked up to speak.

Salem leaped into her arms. "Pilot to copilot. Ready for takeoff!"

"Drink this," Marlin said, handing Sabrina a smoky cup of the potion they'd concocted.

Sabrina sniffed it. *Whew!* Then she held her nose and gulped down the horrid stuff.

"Quickly, everyone!" Zelda commanded. "Gather round them and hold hands!"

Sabrina's new friends gathered round her in a circle of friendship as Zelda invoked the spell:

Dragon's eye and horrid potion,
Work your magic, I implore,
Send my niece and her black kitten,
Back to their true home once more.

"Psst! Sabrina, what does *implore* mean?" Salem whispered.

"You know, 'beg,' 'plead,' stuff like that," she whispered back.

"Gotcha!" He snuggled back down into her arms and crossed his paws for good luck.

Sabrina squeezed her eyes closed. "There's no place like home! There's no place like home!" she muttered, just for good luck, as she hugged Salem to her chest.

For a second nothing happened.

Oh, no. Another failure?

Then Sabrina felt a marvelous tingling wash over her, and she knew Zelda's magic was working.

Seconds later she felt a small jolt, and something about the way the place smelled—or rather, didn't smell!—told her she was home.

But then she heard her aunt Zelda cry out, "Oh, no! What have I done?"

☆

Chapter 12

☆

Sabrina opened her eyes.

For a moment she wasn't sure if the magic had worked or not, because she was still standing in the middle of a medieval village.

Thwang! Three feet to her left, an arrow thunked into a bull's-eye.

And across the grounds she saw Lance the actor throwing down his cape for another young girl.

"We're home!" she cried, hugging Salem. "At least, back at the Medieval Faire just outside Westbridge, where all this began."

Then she looked around and realized she was still surrounded by Zelda, Hilda, Marlin—even Charles!

"What happened?" she asked, totally confused. "Where am I? Am I home or not?"

"You're home," Zelda said, a blush staining her fair cheeks. "But . . . er, we're not."

"Somehow we all traveled through time with you!" Marlin exclaimed. He actually sounded rather excited about it.

Hilda was checking out the cute boys, and Charles stood frozen in absolute terror.

Sabrina looked around at the fairgoers. *What could they possibly be thinking?*

But nobody seemed to be reacting at all. After all, the entire group was dressed in period clothing. And as for Charles . . .

"They must think he's some kind of animated papier-mâché dragon," she whispered to Salem.

But Sabrina had a feeling the ruse wouldn't last for long. "Come on, everybody. Over here!" Sabrina quickly led them down a path into the woods. Then, using a plain old, everyday transporter spell, she zapped them all into the Spellman sisters' living room.

Aunt Zelda—the adult one—crossed her legs and looked up from the scientific journal she was reading on the couch. "Oh, Sabrina. You're home. We were wondering—"

Aunt Zelda spotted the entourage her niece had brought home with her—including the teenage version of herself and her sister Hilda.

Aunt Zelda didn't freak out or shout or faint. She did lay her hand across her forehead for a moment, then slipped off her reading glasses. "Hilda!" she called to the adult version of her sister, who was still in the kitchen. "Would you mind zapping up a pot of coffee? And you'd better make it espresso."

It took a lot of explaining on Sabrina's part, but fortunately Aunt Zelda had centuries of experience in unraveling mixed-up magic and soon had everything sorted out—at least temporarily.

She quickly zapped Charles the dragon with a miniaturization spell and turned him into Sabrina's "new pet lizard," in case some mortal unexpectedly dropped by.

Sabrina helped her aunts get in touch with their "inner child" by talking with their teenage selves about all the issues brewing beneath the stolen necklace situation. Then Zelda used a few bubbling ingredients from her labtop and a sprinkle of magic to blend the two versions of themselves together into one. Zelda wisely noted that when you grow older, you don't change into a different person: the years only add more experience. But the younger "versions" of you are still there, always, in your heart.

The aunts promised to try to remember this truth and listen to that part of themselves a little more often when dealing with their own teenage witch niece.

Marlin—even more mesmerized by the mature Zelda, asked her out on a date—and considered relocating to the future to work in research.

After supper Sabrina went out on her aunts' old Victorian front porch and studied the stars. She was glad to be home, with things sort of back to normal. She certainly had plenty of research for her history paper.

But she couldn't stop thinking about Arthur.

What had become of him? And how come he hadn't been brought into the future with the rest of her friends? Hadn't he joined hands in the circle? She couldn't remember.

And I didn't even really tell him good-bye.

But she told herself it was all for the best. Marlin and Zelda were one thing, but it could never work for a mortal and a half-witch to go out when there was an age difference of a couple of hundred years.

And as for the rest of the world?

It still had its problems. When Sabrina went in for her shift at the coffee house that night, it was pretty much the same old, same old. As she cleared a table near the front door, she shook her head at the mess. There was sugar all over one of the tables, and trash on the floor. At another table, someone had pocketed one of the coffee shop's cute little silver cream pitchers.

Josh told her not to worry. It happened all the time.

Sometime after ten o'clock, things quieted down and the place pretty much emptied out. An old couple sat over in one corner, drinking coffee in companionable silence.

Josh went back in the back room to work on inventory, and Sabrina moped around the café, wiping up tables and putting chairs back where they belonged.

Just as she was wiping down the last table, the bell over the door jingled and somebody came in. Sabrina glanced up to smile and say hello—

And her heart stopped beating.

It was a guy with thick dark hair and shocking blue eyes. He looked so much like . . .

Nah. Couldn't be.

In fact, she frowned when she realized who it really was—one of those college kids from the night before who had skipped out without paying.

"We're closed," Sabrina said harshly.

The guy looked around and saw the old couple in the corner. He smiled. "No, you're not."

Sabrina scowled at his smile. "Those are my grandparents," she fibbed. "They're waiting to take me home."

"I know this place stays open till midnight on Saturdays," he said.

"So where are your friends tonight? Or should I say partners in crime?"

The guy had the decency to blush, Sabrina noted.

It looked good on him.

"They're not my friends anymore," he said quietly.

Sabrina hadn't expected that. "What do you mean?"

"Last night, when we were here? We were all just horsing around, you know? Kidding around and stuff. I didn't know until about an hour ago that our group really stiffed you for the bill."

"Yeah, right," Sabrina said sarcastically.

"Honest," the guy said. "Jeremy left an envelope on the table. He said he'd found some cash after all and left it for you in the envelope along with a big tip. We were late for the movies, so we had to dash out."

"Yeah, they left me an envelope, all right."

The guy nodded. "Jeremy told me what it said."

"So what did you say?"

"I told them all to get lost."

Sabrina was surprised. "Really?"

"Sure. Who needs friends like that? I'd rather go it alone."

Sabrina smiled.

The guy dug into his pocket then and pulled out his wallet. He handed Sabrina some money. "Will this take care of the bill?" he asked. "Plus a good tip?"

It was more than enough. "Sure. This'll cover it."

"Well, gotta go," he said. "Sorry about everything." He turned to leave.

"Hey, wait up a sec," Sabrina called after him.

He turned around and stared at her with those dazzling blue eyes, and Sabrina found herself wondering what he'd look like in a suit of armor.

"So, why'd you come back?" Sabrina asked. "You didn't have to. A lot of kids wouldn't have."

The guy frowned as if he didn't understand the question. "It was the right thing to do. Besides, I was worried you'd get in trouble." He grinned. "I figured you needed a knight in shining armor to come to your rescue."

Sabrina swallowed. Her throat suddenly felt dry.

"Hey, Sabrina!" Josh called as he came out from the back room.

"Uh, yeah, Josh?"

"Things are pretty dead around here. Wanna take off for the night?"

"Sure. Thanks."

Josh grinned at her. "Yeah, see ya."

The guy with the blue eyes was still standing there, his hands stuffed in his pockets. "So, you need somebody to walk you home?"

Sabrina opened her mouth to say she didn't need any help, she could take care of herself.

But what the heck. There were no rules against taking a stroll with somebody. "Sure. Let me get my coat." She quickly got her jacket from the back room, then slipped it on and joined the guy—she didn't even know his name—by the front door.

He held it open for her and she walked through.

"So, what did you say your name was?" she asked.

"Arthur," he said.

"Of course." She shook her head, grinning, as they headed down the street. "I'm Sabrina."

"I know."

"How'd you know?"

He pointed back to the coffee house. "Josh—

that's what you called him, right? He just called you Sabrina."

"Oh yeah." Sabrina blushed at what she had been thinking . . . hoping?

"But . . . you do look familiar. Have I seen you around campus or somewhere?"

Sabrina nodded. "Somewhere . . ."

About the Author

Cathy East Dubowski has written more than 100 books for kids, including the *Sabrina the Teenage Witch* novels *Santa's Little Helper, A Dog's Life, Fortune Cookie Fox,* and *It's a Miserable Life!* plus stories in the Sabrina short-story collections *Millennium Madness* and *Eight Spells a Week.*

Cathy writes in her office in an old converted red barn in North Carolina, where she lives with her husband Mark, daughters Lauren and Megan, two red golden retrievers named Morgan and Macdougal (whose photo appears on *A Dog's Life),* and a guinea pig named Ramona.

Gaze into the future and see what wonders lie in store for Sabrina, The teenage Witch

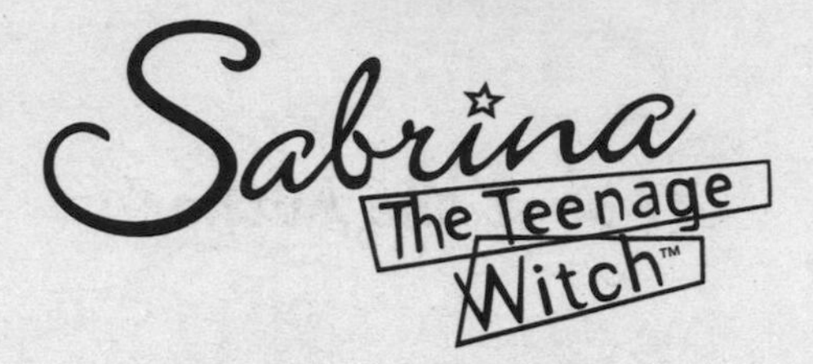

#39 From the Horse's Mouth

Staying on a horse is hard, and learning to ride is even harder. Especially when, for her Phys Ed beginner horseriding class, Sabrina is assigned to ride a cranky and lame critter. His name? Mission Impossible. Uh-oh.

If Sabrina can't learn basic horsemanship in the next two weeks, she'll be saddled with snobby classmate Debra's sniggering – and worse, Sabrina's horse might be sold to a run-down rental stable. There's no time for horsing around. Looks like this might be an impossible mission for Sabrina, until Mission Impossible starts talking!

Don't miss out on any of Sabrina's magical antics – conjure up a book from the past for a truly spellbinding read . . .

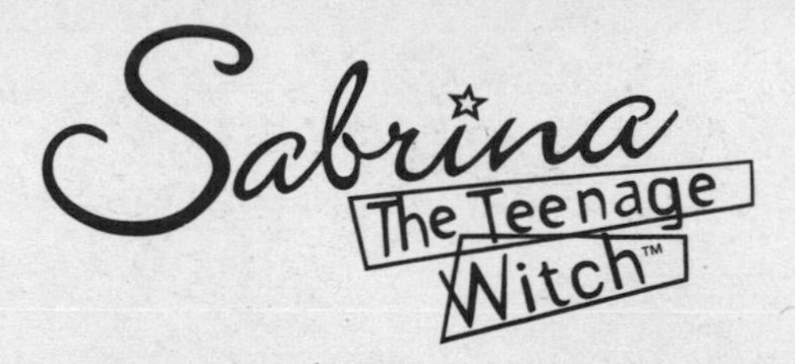

#37 Witch Way Did She Go?

Trying to outsmart her Magic Cue Ball and gain more queries than she's allowed, Sabrina asks it one impossibly long question. The Cue Ball overloads and crashes, and Sabrina and Salem are dropped into the centre of a labyrinth, a giant maze in the Other Realm. Because they both abused the power of the Cue Ball – Salem sneaked in a question on what would happen if he took over the world – now they're stuck in the maze until they find their way out.

To the right? To the left? Down that path? Through this doorway? It's one step at a time as Sabrina and Salem face down a mousetrap, a giant rolling marble and solve Other Realm riddles to reach freedom.